This ~~book~~ *moon* belongs to:

_____

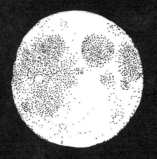

For Mouse and Aura,
my curious cats
—K.K.

Copyright © 2017 by Kim Krans

All rights reserved. Published in the United States by Random House Children's Books,
a division of Penguin Random House LLC, New York.

Random House and the colophon are registered trademarks of Penguin Random House LLC.

Visit us on the Web! randomhousekids.com

Educators and librarians, for a variety of teaching tools, visit us at RHTeachersLibrarians.com

Library of Congress Cataloging-in-Publication Data is available upon request.

ISBN 978-1-101-93227-8 (trade) — ISBN 978-1-101-93228-5 (lib. bdg.) —
ISBN 978-1-101-93229-2 (ebook)

MANUFACTURED IN CHINA

10 9 8 7 6 5 4 3 2 1

First Edition

WHOSE MOON IS THAT?

KIM KRANS

Random House 🏠 New York

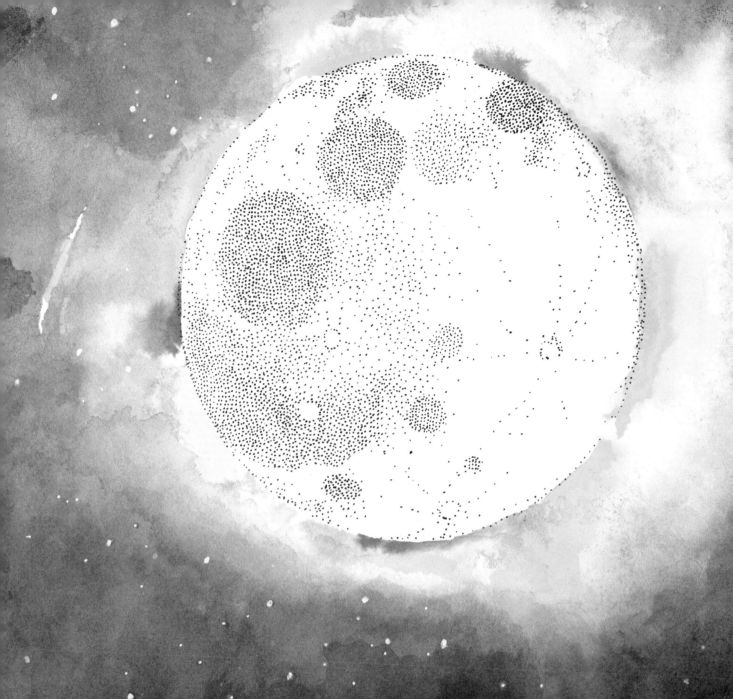

"Whose moon is that?"
asked the curious cat.

"It's my moon!"
said the tree.

"The tree is wrong,"
said the bird with a song.

"The moon belongs to me."

"I found it first!"
said the bear in a burst.
"And I don't like to share."

"Is this a joke?"
The mountain spoke.
"It's mine. It's only fair!"

"Now, that's a lie,"
said the starry sky.

"The moon is held by me."

"It helps me howl,"
    said the wolf with a growl.
"I own it, obviously!"

"Now, I'm appalled,"
the ocean called.
"None of this is true!

"I reflect its light
on my waves all night.
It does not belong to you!"

"All right, all right,"
said the moon so bright.
"If the curious cat must know . . .

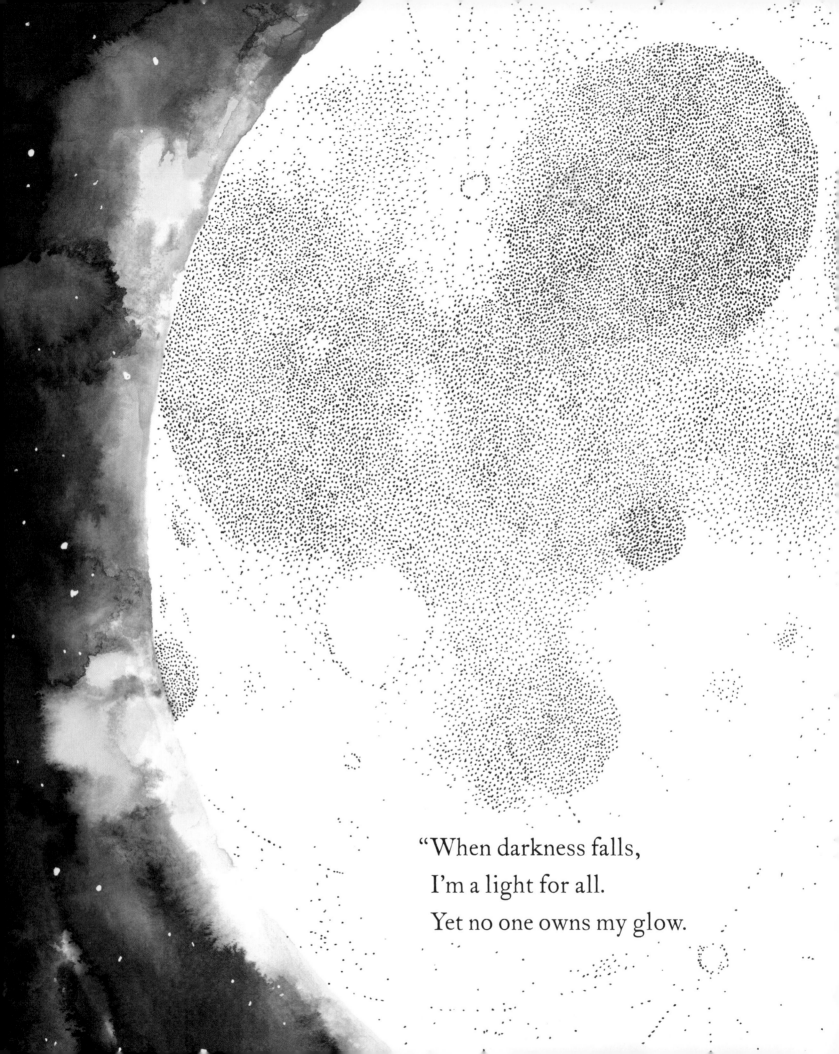

"When darkness falls,
I'm a light for all.
Yet no one owns my glow.

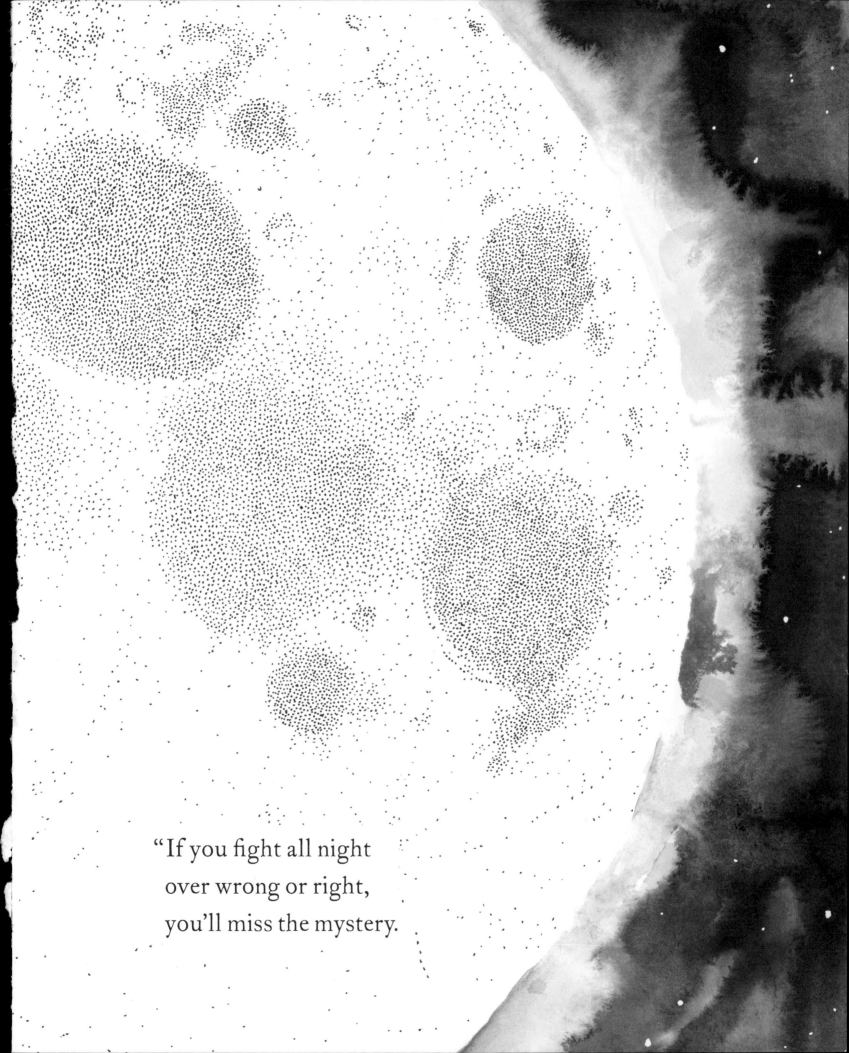

"If you fight all night
over wrong or right,
you'll miss the mystery.

"I shine for one and all,
and none, throughout eternity."

"Whose sun is that?"

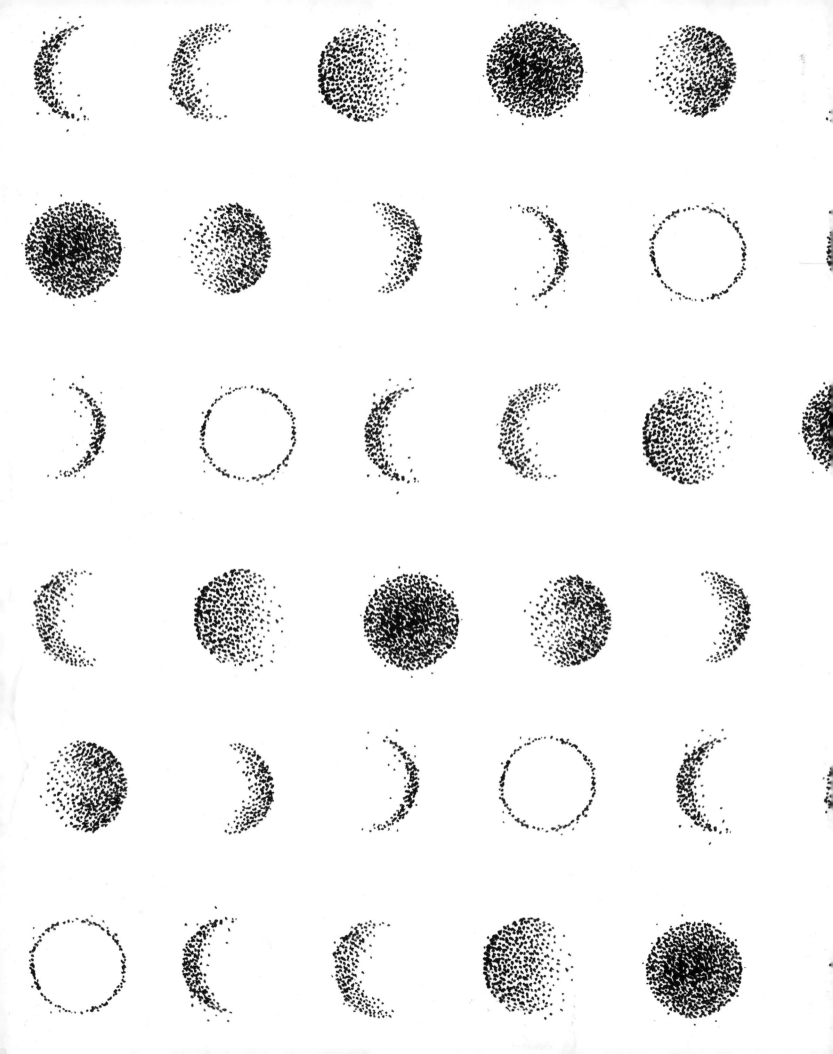